Munay
A Song of Hope
A tale of friendship,
adventure, & courage
Written By H. BEN MEKKI
Illustrations & Inspirations
By Marinda Ooms &
Students
Edited & Published by
H&M Publishers – 2024

While every precaution has been taken in the preparation of this book, the publisher assumes no responsibility for errors or omissions, or for damages resulting from the use of the information contained herein.

MUNAY A SONG OF HOPE

First edition. September 21, 2024.

Copyright © 2024 H. BEN MEKKI.

ISBN: 979-8227757043

Written by H. BEN MEKKI.

Dedication

To my family, who taught me the true meaning of courage and hope. A special thanks to my wife, whose support and creativity were crucial in finishing this book, and to my colleagues and students, whose encouragement and contributions made this journey possible.

Teaser

Abandoned cats. Unexpected friendship. A stage-stealing performance. But when the purrfect meowments come face-to-face with a difficult choice, will love find a way to keep these furry friends where they belong? Find out in this heartwarming tale of friendship, family, and the unbreakable bond between children and their pets.

Chapter I: Golden Days on the Farm

Where golden fields stretched as far as the eye could see, there lived a happy farmer and his lively family.

In the evening, a soft breeze blew through the tall grass, bringing the smell of wildflowers and the sound of chirping crickets. In their cozy house, the warm light from the lamps shone out, inviting everyone passing by to share in the family's joy.

Inside, the farmer's kids were all excited as they gathered around their favorite cat, who was going to have kittens. They were eager, their hearts beating fast with the excitement of new life coming soon. They watched closely as the cat moved around, knowing the babies were almost here.

Actually, Mr. Henderson and his wife had promised their children that they could each choose one kitten to take care of. They made this promise because their neighbor, Mrs. McAllister, had also gotten a new kitten. Her kitten's name was Lily.

"Will it be tonight, Mama?" whispered Hannah, the oldest.

"Shh, Hannah," said her younger brother, Tom. "We don't want to scare her."

Their mom moved quietly among them, calming them down. With gentle words and touches, she told them everything would be fine, "Don't worry, sweetheart. Just let the mama cat do her thing," she said, her hand resting on Hannah's shoulder.

Then, it happened. The mama cat started to give birth, her body moving with each push. The kids held their breath, their eyes wide with wonder as they saw new life being born.

In the soft light of the lamps, it felt like magic. Shadows

danced on the walls, making the room feel even more special. And when the first kitten arrived, a tiny ball of fur, Hannah gasped. "It's a boy!" she cried out. The kids couldn't stop smiling. They laughed and cheered, their hearts full of love for the new babies. Tom reached out to touch the kitten gently. "He's so small," he said in amazement.

Their dad smiled gently, picking up the kitten carefully. "Look at this little guy. His left hind leg is shorter than the rest, just born like that."

"We can call him Limpy!" said Hannah, her eyes shining.

Their mom smiled. "Maybe not, dear. How about Munay?"

"It means the beloved one!" Added the farmer.

"Munay!" they all agreed, liking the name.

The next morning, the kids gathered around the basket full of squirming kittens. Munay, the smallest and most delicate, was snuggled up next to his mom. Munay had a particular charm that set him apart from his siblings. His fur was a soft, downy texture, almost like the finest silk, and it had a unique color that made him stand out. While the other kittens were a mix of common tabby patterns and solid colors, Munay's fur was a gentle mix of pale cream and soft gray, giving him a gentle, special appearance. His coat seemed to shimmer slightly in the morning light, enhancing his delicate look.

Munay's eyes were large and round, an enchanting shade of deep blue that conveyed a sense of curiosity and innocence. They stood out strikingly against his light fur, drawing immediate attention to his tiny face. His ears, still a bit too large for his small head, were always perked up, making him look perpetually alert and curious.

Despite his fragile appearance, there was an obvious warmth to Munay. He often snuggled close to his mother, seeking comfort and security, and his tiny body would gently rise and fall with each of her breaths. His whiskers were long and fine, twitching slightly as he dreamt or reacted to the softest touch.

Munay was a picture of gentle fragility and peaceful beauty, a kitten whose unique appearance and tender disposition made him stand out in the most delightful way.

When Tom reached out to touch Munay's fur, he could feel the kitten's slight, delicate form beneath his fingers. Munay responded to the touch with a soft, contented purr, his little body vibrating with the sound. Munay acted a little differently than his energetic siblings; he was calmer, exuding a quiet grace that was immediately endearing.

"He's so cute!" said Tom. "He looks a bit different, though," Tom noticed, reaching out to touch Munay's soft fur.

Their parents exchanged a look, happy to see the kids loving the new kitten. "Don't worry, Tom," their dad said. "All kittens are different. Munay's leg might be smaller, but he's just as special."

"We'll take care of them," said Tom, determined.

"And I'll make them a cozy bed," added Hannah.

Their dad smiled. "That's a good idea. But remember, kittens need a lot of care. You have to be gentle, especially with Munay."

"We will, Dad!" they said together, feeling confident.

Their dad smiled proudly, knowing they meant it. "Okay then," he said, ruffling their hair.

And so, in the peaceful countryside, surrounded by fields

of gold, a new chapter began for the farmer's family. A chapter filled with love, laughter, and the promise of new adventures to come.

Chapter II: Munay's Struggle

The sunny days of summer stretched into weeks, and before Munay knew it, it was time for Hannah and Tom to go back to school. Munay missed playing with them every day. He wasn't used to being around so many other animals. School kept Hannah and Tom busy learning new things and playing with their friends, so they didn't have as much time to cuddle with Munay all day. Even though the farmer and his family were kind, Munay sometimes felt a little lonely.

The kittens are now more lively and playful, chased after each other, their tiny bodies tumbling through the hay. Munay thrived in the loving embrace of his family. His mother, a gentle tabby with wise eyes and a heart full of love, watched over him with tender care.

Yet, despite the warmth and love that surrounded him, Munay's ears drooped, and a shiver ran down his tiny spine made him feel sad. Try as he might to keep up with his siblings, his physical limitations always seemed to hold him back. He longed to run and play like the other kittens, but his short leg made every movement a struggle.

Munay watched his brothers and sisters frolic in the sunshine. A sense of loneliness crept into his heart. No matter how much love and affection he received from his family, Munay couldn't help but feel like an outsider, forever separated from the carefree happiness that seemed to come so easily to his siblings.

With each passing day, the weight of his disability bore heavily upon him. Munay would often find himself gazing at his reflection in the mirror, his mismatched eyes reflecting the confusion and sadness that churned within his heart. "Why can't I be like them?" he would whisper to his own image, his voice heavy with longing.

Born with a handicapped short left hind leg, Munay had to work harder to keep up with his siblings. His steps were labored, his movements clumsy, as he struggled to keep pace with his siblings. Every jump and run was made harder by the constant reminder of his handicapped leg, a cruel reminder of the limitations that held him back. "Come on, Munay!" Hannah called, her voice laced with concern. "We're playing tag!"

Munay tried, his little legs pumping furiously. But just as he was about to reach them, he stumbled, tumbling into a pile of hay.

Tears welled up in his eyes as he lay there, feeling defeated. Suddenly, he felt a warm wet nudge against his cheek. It was his mother, her eyes filled with understanding. "You'll get there, Munay," his mother would say, her voice a gentle melody of hope and encouragement. "You're stronger than you think."

But no matter how many times his mother reassured him, the echoes of cruel taunts and jeers lingered in his ears. From the farmyard to the fields, Munay was met with teasing laughter and hurtful remarks, his heart bruised by the sting of rejection. "Look at Munay, he can't even run properly!" sneered one of the farm dogs, his words cutting deep into Munay's fragile heart.

Even his own siblings, once his closest companions, seemed to distance themselves from him, their playful banter now tinged with an air of superiority. "Why don't you just give up, Munay?" taunted his brother, a mischievous glint in his eye. "You'll never be like us."

And so, in the quiet solitude of the countryside, Munay

found himself struggling with feelings of self-doubt and loneliness. Each painful remark and cruel jibe served to further isolate him, until he felt like a solitary figure adrift in a sea of indifference. However, despite the darkness that threatened to consume him, Munay clung to a flicker of hope, a beacon of light among the growing darkness.

Chapter III: Whispers of Adventure

One calm evening, Munay found himself alone in the garden. He sat underneath the shade of a large oak tree, his look fixed on the fluttering butterflies dancing in the sunlight.

Munay shocked, his gaze snapping away from the butterflies as a delicate voice startled him "Why are you all alone, Munay?" It was Lily, the neighbor's cat, her eyes filled with curiosity.

Lily was an agile Siamese cat with striking blue eyes that shone with kindness. Her fur was a smooth, creamy color with chocolate-brown points on her ears, face, paws, and tail, giving her a sophisticated appearance. Her slim body moved with an elegance that appeared easy, and her whiskers twitched slightly as she observed Munay.

Munay hesitated, a lump forming in his throat. "I can't play with the others," he muttered, his voice barely a whisper.

Lily sat down next to him, her smile warm and reassuring. "That doesn't mean you can't have fun," she said. "Look at those butterflies. Can you imagine if you could fly like them?"

Her words were accompanied by a gentle purr, a sound that always seemed to relieve those around her. Lily's presence was calming, and her empathetic nature made her an easy confidante. Lily nudged Munay gently with her nose. Her eyes encouraged him to look up and see the beauty she saw in the world.Munay 's eyes widened with wonder. He'd never thought of it that way.

"Maybe not," Lily continued, "but you can still appreciate their beauty. You just have to be a bit more creative, Munay. You can find your own way to have fun, your own way to be special."

Her words sparked a flicker of hope within him. Maybe

Lily was right. Maybe he didn't have to be exactly like his siblings to be happy. A small smile tugged at the corner of his mouth. He looked back at the butterflies, their wings catching the sunlight like stained glass.

Munay watched sadly as his siblings, all sleek and swift, chased butterflies across the golden meadow. He longed to join them, to feel the wind in his fur as he leaped and bounded, but his injured leg held him back. As usual, only Lily, his quiet, thoughtful neighbor, stayed by his side.

"Don't worry, Munay," she purred, nuzzling him gently. "They'll tire themselves out soon, and then we can have our own adventure."

Munay appreciated Lily 's loyalty. Unlike others, she had never mocked him for his limp. In fact, she'd often run alongside him, adjusting her pace to match his. She understood his struggles, his yearning to push his limits even with his limitations.

" Lily," Munay meowed, his voice barely a whisper. "Do you ever... want to leave?"

Lily 's eyes flickered with a hint of sadness. Unlike the rest, she wasn't as playful or carefree. She seemed to carry a quiet wisdom in her gaze, a yearning for something beyond the familiar fields. "Sometimes," she admitted. "There's a whole world beyond these fields, Munay. A world I've only heard stories about from Mrs. McAllister's elder cat, Mittens."

Munay perked up. Mittens, the graceful Siamese cat who often visited them through a hole in the fence, was a source of endless fascination. He'd regale them with tales of his life in the city, a place that seemed straight out of a fantastical dream.

"He talks about towering buildings that scrape the clouds,"

Lily continued, her voice filled with awe. "Buildings that house entire rooms overflowing with yarn! Fluffy clouds of it in every color imaginable, dangling from the ceiling just begging to be batted around. And some shops," she dropped her voice to a secret whisper, "shops with shelves upon shelves of feathery toys which make you want to chase your tail really fast and have fun!"

Munay's eyes widened. Yarn clouds? Catnip strong enough to induce epic tail chases? The city sounded like a feline paradise compared to the familiar twine balls and dried leaves they played with in the farmyard. "And what about the people?" he asked, his voice brimming with curiosity.

Lily tilted her head thoughtfully. "Mittens says they come in all shapes and sizes," she replied. "Some are kind and gentle, leaving out bowls of milk for strays like us. Others can be a little bit grumpy, but even the busiest ones seem to stop and admire a beautiful calico cat now and then."

A calico cat? Munay glanced at his own grey fur, his ears flattened against his head for a moment. Would he stand out even more in the city? But then he remembered Lily 's words about being special. Maybe his difference could be his strength, a way for him to connect with people in the city.

He looked back at Lily, his eyes filled with newfound determination. " Lily," he meowed, his voice laced with excitement. "What if we left? Together?"

Lily 's eyes widened. "Leave? But where would we go?"

"The city!" Munay declared, the word tasting like freedom on his tongue. "Buildings that touch the sky, crowded streets filled with people, and shops overflowing with supplies."

Lily 's eyes gleamed with a mix of awe and doubt. "It

sounds incredible, Munay. But how would we get there? And what about the rest of the cats? What about Hannah and Tom"

Munay hesitated. Leaving without a goodbye felt wrong, but the thought of being stuck in the fields forever was unbearable. "We could wait until Mrs. McAllister leaves for the city," he suggested, referring to their neighbor. "Her pickup truck is big enough for us to sneak in."

Lily pondered his suggestion for a moment, looking thoughtful. Then, a playful look appeared in her eyes. "That's not a bad idea, Munay," she said with a grin. "But we can't just rely on chance. We have to make a plan."

Over the next few days, Munay and Lily huddled together, devising a daring escape plan. They observed Mrs. McAllister packing her pickup Chevy C/K, meticulously noting the days the truck made its trips to the city market and the specific farm products it carried: crates of ripe vegetables, bushels of freshly picked fruits, and bundles of fragrant flowers. Lily, with her agility and stealth, practiced sneaking into the back of the pickup truck, learning its layout and identifying potential hiding spots.

"We'll need to wait for the perfect moment," Lily whispered, her eyes shining with excitement. "And when it comes, we'll be ready."

Munay, on the other hand, focused on building his strength. He spent his days practicing climbing hay bales, navigating through the barn rafters, and even attempting short sprints on his injured leg. He knew he might not be as fast as his siblings, but he refused to let his limitations hold him back any longer.

Chapter IV: The Daring Escape

The day of Mrs. McAllister's market trip arrived, filling Munay's heart with both excitement and nervousness.

He watched from afar as crates of lettuce were loaded onto the back of the pickup truck. His heart swelled with anticipation for the adventure ahead, yet it also ached at the thought of leaving his loved ones behind.

When dusk settled and Mrs. McAllister locked the back of the Chevy, unaware of the two furry stowaways hidden within, Munay and Lily braced themselves for the daring escape. With a silent exchange of determined glances, they knew they were about to embark on a perilous journey into the unknown.

While Mrs. McAllister was turning away to tend to the last-minute details, Munay seized the moment. With a burst of speed, he darted towards the truck, his heart pounding in his chest. Lily followed close behind, her agile movements like a shadow in the fading light.

But just as Munay reached the tailgate, disaster struck. His handicapped leg gave out beneath him, causing him to stumble and almost fall. For a heart-stopping moment, it seemed as though their carefully laid plans would unravel before they even began.

Mrs. McAllister turned back, alerted by the commotion. Her sharp eyes scanned the area, searching for any sign of trouble. Munay froze, his breath caught in his throat, as he prayed that they hadn't been discovered.

With a final burst of determination, Munay pushed through the pain and managed to scramble into the back of the truck just in time. Lily followed suit, her heart racing with adrenaline as she landed beside him. They exchanged a silent, victorious glance, knowing that they had narrowly escaped detection.

The Chevy rumbled to life and began its journey towards the city lights. Munay and Lily braced themselves for the challenges that lay ahead. They were embarking on a journey into the unknown, leaving behind the safety of their farm for the crowded city market. But they were not alone. Together, they faced the uncertainty of the road ahead, determined to carve out their own destiny.

Munay and Lily curled up together in the back, their fur ruffled by the cool evening breeze. The sky above was awash with hues of pink and gold as the last rays of sunlight dipped below the horizon, casting a warm glow over the rolling fields.

When they traveled farther from the familiar sights and sounds of the farm, Munay's heart raced with excitement and uncertainty. He stole a glance at Lily, her fur bristling against the chill in the air, and felt a pang of concern. "Are you cold?" he asked softly, nudging her closer for warmth.

Lily nodded, her breath forming small clouds in the crisp night air. "A little," she admitted, her voice barely a whisper. "But I'll be alright."

Munay wrapped his tail around her, offering what little comfort he could. "We'll be in the city soon," he reassured her, his voice tinged with hope. "Maybe we'll find some new friends there."

The truck rumbled on. They passed fields dotted with grazing cattle and quaint farmhouses nestled among the trees. Each new sight filled them with wonder and curiosity, as they marveled at the world unfolding before them. "Look at that!" exclaimed Lily, her eyes widening with excitement as they passed a shimmering lake bathed in moonlight.

Munay smiled, his heart swelling with gratitude for the chance to experience such beauty. "It's amazing, isn't it?" he said, his voice filled with awe. "I never knew there was so much to see beyond the farm."

They journeyed deeper into the night. Mrs. McAllister made a pit stop at a gas station, the bright lights illuminating the darkened sky. Munay and Lily peered out from the back of the truck, their eyes wide with curiosity as they watched the hustle and bustle of the city come to life before them.

"I wonder what the city will be like," mused Lily, her voice tinged with excitement and apprehension.

Munay nodded, his heart racing with anticipation. "I don't know," he admitted. "But I hope we'll find some new friends there."

Mrs. McAllister refueled the truck. Munay and Lily pressed close for warmth. Their fur brushing against each other in the chilly night air. Despite the uncertainty of their journey, they knew that as long as they had each other, they could face whatever challenges lay ahead.

With a cough and a sputter, the truck lurched back onto the highway, carrying Lily and Munay closer to the city lights. They clung to the hope that their dreams of acceptance and belonging would soon become a reality.

Chapter V: City Lights

The truck entered the heart of San Antonio, Texas and Lily's excitement grew with each passing moment.

The city was busy, yet it held an old-world charm that seemed frozen in time. Tall buildings with fancy decorated fronts loomed over narrow streets paved with smooth, round stones, their windows adorned with colorful flower boxes. Old cars rumbled past, their engines echoing off the stone walls, while the scent of freshly baked bread filling the air from nearby bakeries.

"Wow, look at all the buildings!" she exclaimed, her eyes wide with wonder as they passed towering skyscrapers and bustling streets lined with shops and cafes.

Munay nodded in agreement, his tail swaying with excitement. "It's so different from the farm," he remarked, taking in the sights with a sense of awe. "But I think we'll fit in just fine."

Their conversation flowed freely as they navigated through the crowded streets, their voices filled with anticipation for the adventure that lay ahead. "Look, there's the market!" Lily exclaimed, pointing excitedly as they approached their destination. "I can't wait to see what it's like!"

Munay smiled, his heart swelling with excitement. "Me too," he agreed, his voice filled with enthusiasm. "Maybe we'll meet some new friends there."

Lily and Munay were immediately enveloped in a whirlwind of sights, sounds, and smells when they entered the crowded market. Stalls lined the streets, overflowing with colorful fruits and vegetables, fragrant flowers, and an array of other goods. The air was alive with the sounds of vendors hawking their wares, shoppers bargaining for the best deals, and the cheerful chatter of people going about their day.

Lily's eyes sparkled with delight as she took in the bustling scene around her. "This place is amazing!" she exclaimed, her voice filled with wonder.

Munay nodded in agreement, his whiskers twitching with excitement. "It's like a whole new world," he remarked, his eyes darting eagerly from stall to stall.

When they made their way through the market, Lily and Munay couldn't help but marvel at the sights and sounds around them.

"It's so wonderful to be here," Lily said, her voice filled with joy as she stole a juicy peach from one of the stalls.

Munay nodded, a smile tugging at the corners of his mouth. "It really is," he agreed, his eyes shining with happiness. "I feel like we belong here."

Their conversation flowed easily as they wandered through the market, their bond growing stronger with each passing moment. They exchanged jokes, and reveled in the simple joy of being together.

Surrounded by the hustle and bustle of the market, a sudden commotion caught their attention. Lily and Munay turned to see a group of street dogs causing trouble, their barks echoing through the crowded streets.

"Uh oh," Lily said, her brow furrowing with concern. "Looks like trouble."

Munay nodded, his gaze flicking nervously towards the dogs. "We'd better be careful," he said, his voice tinged with apprehension. "Let's stick together."

With a nod of agreement, Lily and Munay pressed on, navigating through the throngs of people and stalls with caution. But, just as they moved deeper into the market, the crowd grew denser, and they soon found themselves separated from each other.

"Munay? Munay, where are you?" Lily called out, her voice tinged with panic as she searched frantically for her friend.

But Munay was nowhere to be found. Lost and alone in the complex and confusing market, Lily felt a wave of fear wash over her. She knew she had to find Munay and fast, before it was too late. With a determined glint in her eye, she set off into the crowd, her heart pounding in her chest as she called out his name, her voice a series of frantic meows to human ears.

Lily darted through the crowded streets, her eyes wide with fear. She had been separated from Munay in the chaos, and now she found herself alone and vulnerable. The echoes of taunting laughter still rang in her ears, the memory of the bullying cats sending shivers down her spine.

Chapter VI: An Unexpected Kindness

When she navigated with difficulty through the maze of stalls and vendors, Lily's breath came in ragged gasps. The cold, biting wind whipped through the narrow alleyways, sending a shiver down her spine. She wrapped her arms tightly around herself, trying to ward off the chill, but it was no use. She felt exposed and vulnerable, like a small leaf caught in a fierce storm.

Suddenly, a voice cut through the icy air, startling Lily out of her thoughts. "Hey there, are you okay?"

Suddenly, a voice cut through the icy air, startling Lily out of her thoughts. "Hey there, are you okay?"

Lily, the tabby cat with a medal that had her name engraved on it, looked up with wide, frightened eyes. A twelve-year-old boy, with tousled brown hair and a warm smile, knelt beside her. He had just finished school and was on his way home through a different street than usual, drawn by the noises of the crowded market.

The street he walked on was lined with tall, old buildings, their red bricks weathered by time. Vendors called out to potential customers, their stalls filled with colorful wares. The boy wore a navy blue jacket, his school backpack slung over one shoulder, and his cheeks were rosy from the cold.

Lily meowed softly, her green eyes pleading for help. The boy noticed the medal and gently touched it, reading the name aloud. "Lily, huh? Don't worry, Lily. I'll keep you safe." Gathering Lily into his arms, he felt her cold, shaky body relax slightly against his chest. He zipped his jacket up around her, protecting her from the biting wind. "Let's get you somewhere warm," he murmured, deciding to take her to his home, just a few blocks away.

Meanwhile, on a parallel street, Maya, a twelve-year-old girl with dark, curly hair and kind brown eyes, was making her way home from school. She walked with a slight limp, aided by a knee brace that supported her weak knee. Despite her handicap, she moved with a quiet determination. The street she walked on was quieter, lined with old brick buildings and scattered leaves, painting a picturesque scene of a 90's San Antonio neighborhood and its beautiful riverwalk.

While she was turning a corner, she spotted Munay, a cat with a medal bearing his name, limping slightly and meowing in distress. Maya's heart went out to the injured cat. "Munay," she read softly, recognizing his need for care. She knelt down, her movements careful and gentle, her knee brace creaking slightly.

"It's okay, Munay. I've got you," Maya whispered, her voice soothing as she gently picked him up. Holding him close to her chest, she decided to take him home, where she could tend to his injured leg and keep him safe.

As fate would have it, Maya and the boy lived on the same street, their houses just a few doors apart. The street was in Kenwood neighborhood of San Antonio, with white picket fences, some weathered with time, others freshly painted, demarcated the property lines. Two-story houses, a mix of architectural styles from Craftsman bungalows to Spanish Colonial revivals, stood proudly, each with its own unique charm.

They both walked home, each cradling a rescued cat in their arms, their paths destined to cross.

When they finally met, it was outside their houses. The boy, with Lily safely tucked inside his jacket, saw Maya with

Munay and smiled. "Hey," he greeted, his blue eyes sparkling with a mix of warmth and curiosity.

"Hi," Maya replied, her cheeks flushing slightly as she looked at him. She admired how gentle he seemed, a boy she had always noticed but never really talked to.

"What do you have there?" the boy asked, nodding towards Munay.

"This is Munay. I found him lost and hurt," Maya explained, her eyes shining with a mix of concern and affection for the cat in her arms. "And you?"

"This is Lily. She was trembling and alone in the market. I thought I'd bring her home," he replied.

They both smiled at each other, feeling a connection over their shared compassion for the animals. "Well, I guess we both have new friends," Maya said softly.

"Yeah, I guess we do," the boy replied, holding Lily a little closer to shield her from the cold. They exchanged one last look, a silent understanding passing between them, before heading into their respective homes.

Inside the boy's house, his mother greeted him with a warm smile. "Liam, who's this?" she asked, noticing the bundle in his arms.

"This is Lily, Mom. I found her in the market. Can we keep her?" Liam asked, his eyes hopeful.

His mother took a closer look at the shivering cat and nodded. "Of course, we can keep her. Let's get her warmed up and fed."

In the meantime, Maya entered her own home, where her father was reading a newspaper in the living room. "Dad, look who I found," she said, holding Munay up for him to see.

"Well, isn't he a handsome fellow?" her father said, setting the newspaper aside. "What's his name?"

"Munay. He's hurt, but I think he'll be okay with some care," Maya said, her voice filled with determination.

Her father smiled warmly. "I'm sure he will be. Let's get him settled in."

Maya's father gently stroked Munay 's fur when he spoke. "Munay, you see, is not hurt. He was born with his leg like that," he explained, his voice soft and reassuring. "And it seems like Maya has a similar condition with her knee being born weak."

Maya nodded, her heart feeling a connection with Munay while she was looking at his unique leg. "We can understand each other, Munay," she whispered, offering him a tender smile.

Chapter VII: New Friends?

When they entered Maya's room, Munay looked around with curiosity. The room was cozy, with soft pastel-colored walls decorated with posters of kittens and puppies. A fluffy rug lay on the floor, and a comfortable bed was nestled in one corner.

Maya gently placed Munay on her bed, surrounding him with plush pillows for comfort. "This is your new home, Munay," she said softly, her eyes filled with warmth.

Maya settled beside Munay, she gently stroked his fur, finding comfort in his presence before she began to share her story.

" Munay," Maya began, her voice soft and filled with emotion, "I want to tell you about my mom." She paused, happy and sad memories of her mother flooding her mind, all mixed together like a bittersweet melody.

"She was the kindest person I've ever known," Maya continued, her eyes misting with tears. "She used to read me bedtime stories every night and tuck me in with the warmest hug."

With each word, Maya's voice shook a little, her heart heavy with the weight of loss. "But one day, she got sick," she whispered, her breath catching in her throat. "And no matter how hard we tried, we couldn't make her better."

While Maya was speaking, Munay curled up closer, his comforting presence a silent reminder that she was not alone in her pain. Maya took a deep breath, her voice steadying just as she shared memories of her mother - her laughter, her warmth, the way her eyes sparkled with love.

"And then she was gone," Maya whispered, her voice barely above a whisper. "And I didn't know how to go on without her."

Big tears spilled from Maya's eyes as she shared her feelings with Munay. It felt like a giant rock was sitting on her heart, so heavy she could barely breathe. But when she spoke, she felt a sense of release, as if sharing her pain with Munay lifted a burden from her soul.

"And then there's school," Maya confessed, her voice tinged with anger. "The other kids can be so cruel sometimes. They laugh at me because of my weak knee, call me names like 'limpy' or 'wobble legs.'"

Munay purred and snuggled against Maya's leg. It was like a warm hug, helping to ease her sadness. Maya closed her eyes, allowing herself to feel the warmth of Munay 's presence, the comfort of his silent companionship.

"But you know what, Munay?" Maya said, a flicker of determination lighting up her eyes. "I won't let their words break me. I won't let them define who I am."

With each word, Maya felt a newfound strength coursing through her veins, a resolve to rise above the cruelty of others and embrace her own worth. And as she looked into Munay 's eyes, she knew that together, they would face whatever challenges life threw their way, side by side, paw in hand.

A sudden inspiration welled up inside her, and Maya began to sing, her voice soft and trembling at first, then growing stronger and more confident. It was a song she had created herself, a song of hope that encapsulated her journey, her pain, and her dreams.

Her voice filled the room, warm and pure, resonating with a deep emotion that touched Munay 's heart. The song spoke of her struggles, her weak knee, the loss of her mother, and the cruelty she faced at school. Yet, through every verse, a thread of hope wove its way, lifting the melody into something beautiful.

In the first verse, she sang of her mother's love, describing the warmth and safety she felt in her embrace:

"In her arms, I found my light,

In her eyes, the stars so bright.

But shadows fell and took her away,

Leaving me in disarray."

Tears glistened in Maya's eyes, but her voice remained steady, filled with a quiet strength.

The second verse spoke of her own struggles, the way her leg had always set her apart, and the loneliness that came with it:

"With every step, a stumble, a fall,

Laughter echoing down the hall.

But I won't let them break my stride,

In my heart, there's strength inside."

Her voice soared higher, carrying with it the weight of her determination and resilience. Munay watched her carefully, his eyes reflecting a deep understanding.

The chorus brought a shift in tone, filled with a hopeful resolve, as she sang of finding her own path and embracing who she was:

"I'll rise above, I'll find my way,

Through the darkest night, into the day.

With every breath, I'll sing my song,

In this world, I will belong."

Maya's voice filled the room with a powerful resonance, each note a declaration of her inner strength and unyielding spirit.

In the final verse, she sang of Munay, her new companion,

and the bond they shared. She sang of how he helped her find hope again, how together they would face the world:

"Now I've found a friend so true,

In your eyes, I see it too.

Together, we'll walk this land,

Side by side, we'll make our stand."

I'll rise above, I'll find my way,

Through the darkest night, into the day.

With every breath, I'll sing my song,

In this world, I will belong.

The song came to an end and the room seemed to thrum with the fading melody, the air charged with the raw emotion of her journey. Munay let out a soft meow, his gratitude and affection clear in his eyes.

Maya felt a weight lift from her heart, a sense of cleansing feeling washing over her. She had shared her deepest pain and her highest hopes, and in doing so, she had found a new sense of peace.

Looking at Munay, she smiled through her tears. "Thank you, Munay," she whispered. "Thank you for listening."

And in that moment, in the quiet of her room, Maya felt that she was no longer alone.

Darkness draped the world in its inky cloak, the cozy homes became beacons of warmth and light. Munay and Lily lay in their respective beds, each nestled in warmth and comfort. Munay curled up on Maya's bed, the soft blanket cocooning him, while Lily sprawled luxuriously on a cushioned chair in Liam's room. The gentle hum of the night, punctuated by the occasional rustle of leaves outside, lulled them into a peaceful slumber. The sense of safety and love from their humans surrounded them like a protective shield.

Chapter VIII: Maya and Liam

The next morning, the sun rose, casting a golden glow over the neighborhood. Birds chirped merrily, and a light breeze carried the scent of blooming flowers. It was a shiny, beautiful day, filled with promise.

In her room, Maya got ready for school, the sunlight streaming through her window and dancing on the walls. She hummed a tune, her heart light despite the challenges she knew she would face. Munay watched her intently, his eyes following her every movement. Maya slipped her backpack over her shoulder and bent down to give Munay a gentle scratch behind his ears.

"Be good, Munay," she whispered. "I'll be back before you know it."

Next door, Liam was packing his own school bag, making sure he had everything he needed for the day. Lily stretched lazily on the chair before hopping down and rubbing against Liam's legs. He chuckled, bending down to pat her head.

"See you later, Lily. Take care of yourself, okay?" he said with a grin.

When Maya and Liam met outside and started their walk to school, Munay jumped onto the windowsill, peering through the glass. His soft, plaintive meow caught Maya's attention. She turned, waving at him with a bright smile.

"Goodbye, Munay! I'll see you later," she called out, her voice filled with affection.

Munay watched them until they disappeared around the corner. Then, using a small jump with all his might, he leaped down from the window and headed to the back door. He had an idea.

Meanwhile, in Liam's house, Lily had a similar thought.

She slipped out the back door, which was open just a crack, and padded into the yard, her whiskers twitching with curiosity.

Munay and Lily ventured out and met in the street between their homes. The morning air was crisp and filled with tiny drops of water on the grass. Munay 's eyes sparkled just as he saw Lily approaching. Lily let out a friendly chirp, and they touched noses in greeting.

Munay's tail flicked with excitement as he gazed at Lily. "Good morning, Lily! Glad to find you. How are you, and how was that boy?"

Lily purred softly, her whiskers twitching with amusement. "Likewise, happy to find you Munay. Liam's home is so cozy, and the boy took good care of me. How about you? How was your night with Maya?"

"It was wonderful," Munay replied, his eyes shining. "Maya is so kind and gentle. I feel so lucky to have found her."

Lily nodded in agreement. "Liam is the same. We're fortunate to have such loving humans."

Munay stretched, his back arching gracefully. "I wonder what they'll do at school today."

Lily's ears perked up. "Do you think they have fun there? Or is it all about learning and being serious?"

Munay tilted his head thoughtfully. "Maya mentioned something about an end-of-year show. It sounds like it could be fun, but she's worried about participating."

"Why would she be worried?" Lily asked, her eyes wide with curiosity.

Munay sighed, his tail flicking. "She has a weak leg. Some of the other kids make fun of her for it. It's so unfair."

Lily's fur bristled with indignation "That's awful!"

Munay added: "Maya is so brave for wanting to join the show despite everything. I wish there was something we could do to help her."

Lily thought for a moment, her eyes narrowing in determination. "Maybe just being there for them, like they are for us, is enough. Our love and support can make a big difference."

Munay nodded, his resolve strengthening. "You're right, Lily. We'll always be there for them."

The cats sat together in the quiet street closeby the front yard of Maya's home. The bond between Munay and Lily grew stronger. They knew they had found true friends in each other and in their humans. The morning sun continued to rise, casting a warm glow over their small world, filled with hope and friendship.

At school, the hallways buzzed with the chatter of students, their laughter and conversations echoing off the shiny floors and brightly decorated walls. The smell of fresh paint mixed with the leftover smell of breakfast from the cafeteria. Maya moved through the sea of students, her eyes focused ahead, determined not to let the day's upcoming challenges break her spirit.

After the morning class, the bell rang for break time. Maya made her way to her usual spot in the schoolyard, a bench beneath an old oak tree that provided a bit of shade and solitude. She was unwrapping her sandwich when the familiar sound of unfriendly laughter reached her ears. The group of girls who had tormented her for weeks was approaching, their expressions filled with meanness.

"Look who's still dreaming about that show," one of them

sneered, her voice dripping with sarcasm.

"Yeah, Maya, you should just stick to watching from the sidelines," another added, her tone cruel.

Maya tried to ignore them, focusing on her sandwich, but they wouldn't stop. One of the girls shoved her shoulder, causing her to lose her balance and stumble off the bench. As she fell, her heart pounded with a mix of fear and frustration.

"Do you really think you can stand on stage with that leg?" one of the girls taunted. "You'll just embarrass yourself and everyone else."

"Yeah, nobody wants to see you trip and fall during the performance," another chimed in, laughing.

Maya clenched her fists, holding back tears. "You don't know what I'm capable of," she said, her voice shaking but defiant.

"Oh, we know exactly what you're capable of," the first girl shot back. "And it's not much."

Just then, Liam, who had been passing by, witnessed the entire scene. His eyes flashed with anger as he rushed over, helping Maya to her feet.

"Leave her alone!" Liam shouted, his voice firm and unhesitating. "Maya has every right to be here and to participate in the show if she wants to."

The girls smirked, but as they noticed more people watching and saw how firmly Liam stood his ground, they stepped back, quietly whispering to each other as they left.

Maya looked up at Liam, her eyes shining with gratitude. "Thank you," she whispered, her voice filled with emotion.

Liam smiled warmly, offering her a reassuring nod. "Anytime, Maya. Don't let them get to you. You're stronger than they know."

Together, they walked back toward their classrooms. The school was a bustling hive of activity, with students bustling to and from classes, teachers calling out reminders, and the distant hum of lessons being conducted. As they walked, the sun streamed through the large windows, casting patterns of light and shadow on the tiled floors.

The day continued with lessons, but Maya's mind was set on one goal. After the final bell rang, signaling the end of classes, she made her way to Mrs. Bennett's classroom. The room was quiet now, filled with the remaining scent of chalk and the soft rustle of papers.

"Mrs. Bennett," Maya began, her voice shaking slightly but filled with determination, "I know some people think I can't do it because of my leg, but I really want to be in the end-of-year show. I've been practicing, and I believe I can do it."

Mrs. Bennett looked up from her desk, her kind eyes meeting Maya's. She walked around to sit beside her student, the weight of her understanding and empathy evident in her gaze.

"Maya, I've seen how hard you work and how passionate you are about performing," Mrs. Bennett said gently. "Tell me more about why you want to be in the show."

Maya took a deep breath. "It's not just about proving the other girls wrong," she said, her voice steadying. "It's about proving to myself that I can do it. I love singing and dancing, and I want to share that with everyone, despite my leg. I want to show them that I'm more than my weakness."

Mrs. Bennett nodded thoughtfully. "That's a beautiful reason, Maya. And I believe you have the talent and the determination to succeed. It won't be easy, and you'll need to practice even harder, but I'm here to support you every step of the way."

Maya's eyes lit up with hope. "Thank you, Mrs. Bennett. I'm ready to work as hard as it takes."

Encouraged by her teacher's support, Maya felt a surge of hope. She left the classroom with a renewed sense of purpose. The school's corridors seemed brighter, the challenges ahead less daunting. With the support of friends like Liam, the comfort of Munay, and her own steady spirit, she was ready to face whatever challenges lay ahead.

Chapter IX: A Song of Unity

While walking home, the sky was painted with hues of orange and pink, the setting sun casting a warm glow over everything. Maya knew that each day would bring its own battles, but with her newfound strength and the support around her, she was ready to rise above them. Especially now that her new neighbor, Liam, was becoming a close friend.

He was brave and gentle, and Maya felt a burst of joy at the thought of having him nearby. Liam and his mother had moved into the neighborhood only last month, and he already felt like a source of strength for her.

When Maya walked down the familiar street where she had first found Munay, she was lost in her thoughts. To her surprise, she saw Liam coming towards her, his face lighting up with a big smile when he saw her. It seemed like a special coincidence that the two best friends she had now, Liam and Munay, were both found on this same street.

"Hey, Maya!" Liam called out, waving.

"Hi, Liam," Maya replied with a smile, her heart feeling a bit lighter.

They walked side by side, their footsteps in sync as they headed towards their neighborhood. The trees lining the street rustled gently in the breeze, and The sun was getting low in the sky, painting the world with a warm, orange glow.

"Thank you for what you did today," Maya began, her voice sincere. "Standing up to those girls meant a lot to me."

Liam shrugged modestly. "It was nothing, really. No one should be treated like that, especially not you. I'm glad I was there."

"It wasn't nothing to me," Maya insisted. "It was brave, and it showed me that I have a friend who believes in me."

Liam smiled warmly. "Well, you do. And you know, you're stronger than you think. Don't let anyone tell you otherwise."

"So, how was your day?" Maya asked, eager to keep the conversation going.

"It was good," Liam said. "I've been practicing the piano a lot, trying to get ready for the school's end-of-year show."

"Really? That's amazing!" Maya's eyes sparkled with interest. "What are you going to play?"

"Actually, I'm still trying to figure that out," Liam admitted. "I'd love to put together a team—maybe someone to sing, someone to dance. I think a collaborative performance would be incredible."

Maya's heart skipped a beat. "I love to sing. It's been a dream of mine to perform in the show."

Liam's face lit up. "That's perfect! We should team up! You sing, I'll play the piano, and maybe we can find a dancer. What do you think?"

"I'd love that!" Maya said, her excitement growing. "But... you know how some kids can be."

"Yeah, I saw what happened today," Liam nodded sympathetically. "But don't let them stop you. You have a beautiful voice, Maya. You should definitely sing."

As they walked, their conversation drifted from school to their ambitions and dreams. They discovered that they shared a lot of common interests, and Liam's encouragement made Maya feel more confident about her decision to participate in the show.

Suddenly, something caught Liam's eye. "Hey, Maya, look at that!"

Maya followed his gaze and saw Munay and Lily playing

together in the front yard of her home. They were chasing each other around, their tails flicking playfully in the air.

"Isn't that adorable?" Maya said, laughing.

"Yeah, they look like they're having the best time," Liam agreed.

They both noticed the medals hanging from the cats' necks. "Wait a minute," Maya said, stepping closer. "Those medals look exactly the same!"

Liam leaned in for a better look. "You're right! How weird is that?"

"It's like they were meant to find each other," Maya mused.

Maya's father stepped out onto the porch and called to her. "Maya, it's time to come inside, sweetheart."

"Okay, Dad!" she replied. Turning to Liam, she smiled. "Thanks for walking with me. I had a great time."

"Me too," Liam said. "I'll see you tomorrow at school. And hey, maybe you can come over this weekend? I'd love to show you my piano."

"I'd love that," Maya said. "See you tomorrow, Liam."

"See you tomorrow, Maya," Liam replied with a grin.

Maya and Liam parted ways and both felt a sense of anticipation for the days to come. Their newfound friendship, along with the bond between Munay and Lily, made everything seem brighter. And with the promise of a new adventure at Liam's house, Maya felt a surge of excitement. She was ready to face whatever challenges came her way, supported by her friends and her father.

Chapter X: Beyond the Steps

Maya and Liam's friendship bloomed like wildflowers, untamed and vibrant, filling the emptiness in each other's lives. After school and on weekends, they found themselves drawn to each other, eager to share moments of laughter and understanding. As they spent more time together, their bond deepened, filling the lonely spaces inside them with warmth and companionship.

"Hey, Maya, do you want to come over and listen to me play the piano?" Liam asked one afternoon, his eyes bright with excitement.

"Sure, Liam! I'd love to," Maya replied, her face lighting up with a smile. "Your piano playing is amazing!"As they entered Liam's house, Maya watched in awe as he sat at the piano, his fingers dancing across the keys with ease. The music that filled the room was enchanting, wrapping around Maya like a warm embrace.

"Wow, Liam, your playing is incredible!" Maya exclaimed, her eyes sparkling with admiration.

Liam beamed with pride. "Thanks, Maya! I've been practicing a lot lately."

Just then, Liam's mother entered the room, her warm smile lighting up her face. "Hello, Maya, it's lovely to meet you. I'm Liam's mom, Mrs. Thompson."

Maya returned the smile, feeling instantly welcomed. "Nice to meet you, Mrs. Thompson. Thank you for having me over."

"It's our pleasure, Maya," Mrs. Thompson replied. "Would you and Liam like some cookies? I just baked a fresh batch."

Maya's eyes lit up with excitement. "Yes, please! That sounds delicious."

Liam grinned at Maya. "My mom's cookies are the best. You're in for a treat!"

With that, Mrs. Thompson disappeared into the kitchen, leaving Maya and Liam to enjoy the music and each other's company.

Inspired by the music, Maya couldn't resist the urge to dance. Despite the constant reminder of her handicapped leg, she moved with grace and determination, her movements fluid and expressive.

With each step, Maya felt the rhythm of the music coursing through her veins, washing away any doubts or fears. She focused on the melody, letting it guide her as she twirled and spun, her body moving in sync with the music.

"Wow, Maya, you're an amazing dancer," Liam exclaimed, his eyes wide with wonder as he watched her twirl and spin.

"Thanks, Liam," Maya replied, her cheeks flushing with embarrassment. "Dancing has always been a passion of mine."

As Maya danced, Munay and Lily watched from their perch, their tails twitching with curiosity. Sensing Maya's joy, they exchanged a glance and shared a silent agreement. It was time to help their friend.

"Come on, Lily," Munay whispered, nudging his sister gently. "Let's join Maya and show her she's not alone."

With a flick of their tails, Munay and Lily leaped from their perch and joined Maya on the dance floor. Together, they moved in perfect harmony, their movements mirroring Maya's with grace and precision.

"Look, Maya, Munay and Lily are dancing with you!" Liam exclaimed, his eyes wide with amazement.

Maya's heart swelled with gratitude as she danced with her

newfound friends. Despite her challenges, she knew she wasn't alone. With Liam's music filling the air and Munay and Lily by her side, she felt like she could conquer the world.

When the sun began its descent, casting hues of orange and pink across the sky, Maya and Liam found themselves seated together on the porch, enveloped in the peaceful hush of the evening. The air was filled with a sense of serenity, yet beneath the surface lay a flood of emotions waiting to be unearthed.

With a heavy heart, Maya began to speak, her voice barely above a whisper. "I miss her every day," she confessed, her gaze fixed on the horizon.

"When she got sick, it was like... like a piece of me was taken away."

Liam listened carefully, his heart aching for his friend. "I can't imagine how hard that must have been for you, Maya," he murmured, his voice soft and full of empathy.

Tears welled up in Maya's eyes as memories of her mother flooded her mind. "She was so kind, Liam," she said, her voice trembling with emotion. "Even when she was sick, she always put others first. She was my rock, my guiding light."

Liam reached out, his hand finding Maya's in the dim light of dusk.

"She sounds like an incredible person, Maya," he said, his voice filled with warmth. "And I know she's watching over you, proud of the strong, resilient person you've become."

Maya offered a small smile, grateful for Liam's comforting words. "Thank you, Liam," she whispered, her voice barely audible over the gentle rustle of the evening breeze. "That means a lot to me."

Their conversation shifted, and Liam began to share his

own story. He spoke of his parents' separation, the upheaval it had caused in his life, and the subsequent move to the new town. As he spoke, Maya listened carefully, her heart aching for her friend.

"I felt so lost, Maya," Liam admitted, his voice tinged with sadness. "Leaving everything behind, starting over in a new place... It was like I was a boat, with no anchor to hold me steady."

Maya nodded in understanding, her own experiences of loss and upheaval resonating deeply with Liam's words. "I'm sorry you had to go through that, Liam," she said softly, her voice filled with empathy. "But I'm glad you're here now. You've brought so much light into my life."

They sat together in companionable silence, while the evening drew to a close, the fading light of dusk casting long shadows across the porch and with Munay and Lily nestled at their feet.

Liam's mother stepped onto the porch, a warm smile on her face. "Come on, kids. Dinner's getting cold," she gently urged, holding the screen door open for them.

Maya and Liam rose from their seats, and as they did, Munay and Lily stretched and followed suit. Maya glanced down at the cats, their presence a comforting reminder of the bond they all shared. She gave Liam's hand one last squeeze before releasing it.

"Thanks for listening, Liam," Maya said, her voice soft but filled with gratitude.

"Anytime, Maya," Liam replied with a smile. "Let's go have some dinner."

Chapter XI: A Dance of Determination

The end-of-year show approached and excitement filled the air. The school buzzed with talk of performances, costumes, and rehearsals. In the midst of this frenzy, Maya and Liam made a big decision—they would team up for the show. Maya would dance and sing, while Liam would play the piano.

"Are you sure you're okay with dancing and singing?" Liam asked Maya one afternoon as they sat in the school cafeteria.

Maya nodded, her eyes shining with determination. "I know it won't be easy, but I really want to do this. Besides, with you playing the piano, I know we can make it amazing."

Liam smiled, feeling a warm sense of camaraderie. "Alright then. Let's give it our all."

Before deciding on their plans, Maya and Liam tried to approach some girls to see if anyone would team up with them for the dance. They hoped to form a small group that could enhance their performance.

During lunch, Liam and Maya walked up to a group of girls chatting by the lockers. "Hey, we're looking for someone to join our team for the show. Would any of you be interested?" Liam asked, trying to sound enthusiastic.

One girl glanced at Maya's leg and then quickly looked away. "Um, sorry, I already have a team," she mumbled, avoiding eye contact.

Another girl shrugged, "Yeah, me too. And we're kinda full already."

Maya felt a pang of disappointment but tried to stay positive. "No worries. Thanks anyway!"

They approached a few more girls, but the responses were similar. Some had already formed their teams, while others seemed hesitant or reluctant to join a group with Maya. One girl even said, "I think you guys will do great on your own. Good luck!" before quickly walking away.

After several unsuccessful attempts, Liam turned to Maya with a determined look. "It looks like it's just us, Maya. Are you still up for it?"

Maya took a deep breath and smiled. "Absolutely. We've got this, Liam."

They started practicing together, both at home and at school. Their practice sessions were filled with hard work, laughter, and the occasional misstep. Munay and Lily often joined in, adding their playful antics to the rehearsals. Munay, with his short leg, danced around with a grace that defied his physical limitation, inspiring Maya every time she saw him.

One afternoon, as they practiced in Maya's living room, Maya suddenly grimaced and stumbled, her weak leg giving out.

Liam immediately stopped playing. "Are you okay, Maya?"

Maya took a deep breath, her face etched with worry. "It's just my leg. It gets so painful sometimes. I feel like it's holding me back."

Munay trotted over, rubbing his head against Maya's ankle. She smiled down at him, comforted by his presence. "You know, Munay never lets his short leg stop him," she said, her voice thoughtful. "He just keeps going, finding ways to move and dance."

Liam nodded, his expression serious. "You're right. Munay's incredible. Maybe we can take some inspiration from him."

Maya's eyes lit up. "I have an idea. What if I incorporate Munay and Lily into the dance? They can be my partners, and I can use my hands and upper body more. That way, I won't have to rely so much on my leg."

Liam grinned. "That sounds amazing. Let's try it."

They began designing a special dance that would allow Maya to use her strengths while minimizing the strain on her leg. Munay and Lily quickly caught on, following Maya's lead as she moved gracefully with her hands and arms, incorporating the cats into her routine. "Okay, let's try this from the top," Maya said, taking a deep breath. She was standing in Liam's living room, which had become their rehearsal space.

The soft afternoon light streamed through the windows, casting a warm glow on the piano and the scattered sheet music.

Liam positioned himself at the piano, his fingers hovering over the keys. "Ready when you are, Maya," he said with an encouraging smile.

Maya nodded and began to move. She stretched her arms out gracefully, her movements fluid and expressive. "I'll start with this sweeping motion," she explained, demonstrating a move that involved a gentle sway of her torso and a graceful sweep of her arms. "This way, I can avoid putting too much pressure on my leg."

"That looks beautiful, Maya," Liam said, playing a soft, pleasant-sounding tune that matched her movements. The melody was uplifting, filled with hope and resilience, echoing the song of overcoming obstacles and finding strength within.

Munay and Lily watched intently, their eyes following every move. When Maya paused, they both leaped into action. Munay, despite his short leg, balanced on his hind legs, mirroring Maya's sweeping motion with his front paws. Lily twirled around, her movements light and playful.

"Look at them!" Maya laughed, her eyes shining with joy. "They're natural dancers!"

"Munay and Lily are really into it," Liam agreed, laughing along. "They're adding a whole new level to our performance."

Maya continued to guide Munay and Lily through the routine. She knelt down, using her arms to create flowing patterns in the air. "This way, I can incorporate more upper body movements," she explained, "and the cats can mimic my motions."

Liam watched, his heart swelling with admiration. "You're doing great, Maya. This is going to be an amazing performance."

Maya smiled, feeling a surge of confidence. "Thanks, Liam. Let's keep practicing."

They spent the next hour perfecting their routine. Maya twirled and spun with her arms, her leg moving only when necessary. Munay and Lily followed her every move, their tails swaying in rhythm with the music.

"Let's add a lift here," Maya suggested, demonstrating how she could lift Munay with one arm while twirling with the other. "It'll add a dramatic flair to the dance."

Liam played a few notes, experimenting with the timing. "I like it," he said. "It'll give the audience a moment to catch their breath."

"Exactly," Maya said, beaming. "And then we can bring it down with a gentle spin, ending with Munay and Lily sitting gracefully on either side of me."

They rehearsed the lift and spin several times, fine-tuning each movement. "Remember, Munay," Maya said, looking into the cat's eyes, "we're in this together. You're my dance partner."

Munay meowed in response, nuzzling her cheek. Lily rubbed against Maya's leg, purring softly.

The music swelled to a crescendo. Maya lifted Munay into the air, spinning gracefully before lowering him gently. She ended with a flourish, her arms extended, Munay and Lily poised elegantly beside her.

"That was perfect," Liam said, his voice filled with awe. "You did it, Maya."

Maya's face lit up with a bright smile. "We did it," she corrected, looking at Munay, Lily, and Liam. "We're a team."

They shared a moment of triumph, the bond between them growing stronger with each practice session. With their unique dance taking shape and the cats adding their charm, Maya felt more confident than ever. The end-of-year show was no longer just a challenge—it was an opportunity to showcase their strength, unity, and creativity.

One day, as they practiced in the school gym, Maya found herself struggling again. Her leg throbbed painfully, and she had to stop.

"I don't know if I can do this," Maya said, tears of frustration welling up in her eyes.

Liam walked over and put a comforting hand on her shoulder. "You're doing great, Maya. Remember, it's okay to take a break. You've come so far already."

Maya looked down at Munay, who was sitting by her feet, watching her with his big, trusting eyes. She knelt down and gently stroked his fur. "Munay, sometimes it feels like my leg is a mountain I can't climb. How do you do it? How do you keep going despite everything?"

Munay looked up at her, his eyes full of understanding. He got up and started to dance, showing her what they practiced together.

With inspiration, Maya wiped her tears away. "If Munay can do it, so can I," she said, determination returning to her voice.

Liam smiled. "That's the spirit. Let's give it another go."

As the days passed, Maya and Liam shared more about their hopes and dreams for the show.

One evening, as they practiced in Maya's backyard, the sun setting behind them in a blaze of colors, Maya turned to Liam. "You know, I think this show is more than just a performance for us. It's a chance to prove to ourselves and everyone else that we can overcome anything."

Liam nodded, his eyes reflecting the same determination. "Absolutely. And with Munay and Lily by our side, we're unstoppable."

The cats meowed in agreement, their tails twitching with excitement. Munay and Lily, sensing the importance of the moment, seemed to understand that they were part of something special.

Later that evening, as they took a break from practicing, Maya and Liam sat on the porch steps. "So, what do you want to do after we finish school?" Maya asked, looking at Liam with curiosity.

Liam thought for a moment, his fingers idly playing a melody on the porch railing. "I've always loved music. I'd love to go to university and study music, maybe even make a career out of it. But I also want to keep my options open. What about you, Maya?"

Maya smiled, her eyes sparkling with excitement. "I love dancing and singing. I think I'd like to study theater or dance at a high level. Maybe even perform professionally someday. But I also want to keep learning. There's so much out there to explore."

Liam nodded, impressed by her ambition. "We could even do both, you know. Study and perform. Imagine us traveling the world, performing in different places, and still learning and growing."

"That sounds amazing," Maya said, her heart swelling with excitement. "We could make a real difference, inspire others with our story."

While Maya and Liam were dreaming about their future, Munay and Lily sat nearby, sharing their own thoughts.

"Do you miss the farm?" Munay asked, his eyes reflecting a mix of emotions.

Lily purred softly, her tail curling around her paws. "Sometimes. I miss the wide-open spaces, the other animals. But I also love being here with Maya and Liam. They need us."

Munay nodded, his heart torn between the past and the present. "It's like we were meant to be here, to help them. Maybe it's our destiny."

Lily leaned against him, offering comfort. "We're happy here, Munay. We're making a difference in their lives. And they love us."

Munay purred in agreement, feeling a sense of purpose. "Yes, we are where we need to be."

Suddenly, Munay noticed a flickering light in the window of Maya's father's bedroom. His ears perked up, catching a strange sound of something falling. Munay's instincts kicked in, and he knew something was wrong.

Munay meowed urgently, tugging at Maya's dress with his teeth.

Maya looked down, confused. "What is it, Munay?"

Munay pulled harder, his eyes filled with worry. It looked like he was saying "Come with me, now!"

Maya jumped up and followed Munay as he darted into the house. Liam, sensing something was wrong, followed closely behind.

They rushed to Maya's father's bedroom, where they found him lying on the floor, unconscious. Maya screamed in fear, her heart pounding in her chest.

"Dad! Dad, are you okay?" she cried, kneeling beside him and trying to shake him awake.

Liam ran to get help, his own heart racing with fear and worry. "Hold on, Maya! I'll get help!"

Chapter XII: The Show Must Go On

The next moments blurred together as the ambulance attendants arrived and rushed Maya's father to the hospital. Liam's mother drove Maya and Liam there, the car ride filled with tense silence. Munay and Lily stayed back at the house, their worried eyes following the car as it sped away.

Maya sat in the back seat, staring out the window, her mind racing with fear and uncertainty.

Liam's mother glanced back at her, her voice soft and soothing. "He's in good hands, Maya. The doctors will take care of him."

Maya nodded, trying to believe her words. She turned to Liam, who sat beside her, his face pale and worried. "Do you think he'll be okay?" she whispered, her voice trembling.

Liam reached over and squeezed her hand. "He's strong, Maya. He'll pull through. And we're here for him, and for you."

The car ride felt interminable, the silence heavy with worry. Maya's thoughts were a jumble of memories and fears. She remembered her mother's illness, how helpless she felt watching her fade away. The thought of losing her father too was unbearable.

Munay and Lily, left behind at the house, paced nervously. Munay meowed softly, looking up at Lily. "Do you think they'll be okay?"

Lily nuzzled him gently. "They're strong, Munay. We have to believe in them."

At the hospital, the sterile smell and bright lights made everything feel even more surreal. Maya clung to Liam's mother, who held her tightly, offering silent comfort. Liam stood close by, his face pale and worried.

"Is he going to be okay?" Maya asked a nurse, her voice shaking.

The nurse gave her a reassuring smile. "We're doing everything we can. The doctors are with him now."

After what felt like an eternity, a doctor finally approached them. His face was calm but serious. "Your father has had a heart attack. We're preparing him for surgery now."

Maya's eyes widened with fear. "Will he be alright?" she asked, her voice barely above a whisper.

The doctor nodded. "We're optimistic. It's good you got him here quickly. He needs a heart operation, and we're confident it will be successful."

Maya bit her lip, trying to hold back her tears. Liam's mother knelt beside her. "Maya, your dad is in good hands. The doctors here are very skilled."

Hours later, the surgery was over. Maya's father was stable, but he needed to stay in the hospital for recovery. Maya sat by his bedside, holding his hand, her heart heavy with worry. The clean hospital smell filled the room, and the soft beeping of the heart monitor was the only sound breaking the silence.

"Dad, please wake up," she whispered, her voice breaking. "I can't lose you too."

She gazed at her father's face, pale but peaceful, hoping for any sign of movement. Tears welled up in her eyes, blurring her vision. She gently squeezed his hand, willing him to respond, feeling the cold, limp touch of his fingers.

Liam and his mother stayed with her, their presence a comforting anchor in the storm of emotions. Liam's mother placed a reassuring hand on Maya's shoulder. "He's strong, Maya. Just like you. He'll get through this."

Liam nodded, sitting on the other side of the bed. "We're here for you, Maya. Every step of the way."

The room was filled with a heavy silence, punctuated only by the rhythmic beeping of the machines. Maya took a deep breath, feeling the weight of the moment. She knew she had to be strong, for her father and for herself.

The next morning, Maya woke up in the hospital room, still holding her father's hand. She felt a gentle touch on her shoulder and looked up to see Liam's mother.

"How are you holding up, sweetheart?" she asked softly.

Maya shrugged, her eyes red from crying. "I don't know. I just... I don't want to lose him."

"You're not going to lose him," Liam's mother reassured her. "He's strong, and he has you to fight for. You've been so brave, Maya."

Just then, the doctor walked in, checking on Maya's father. He smiled at Maya. "He's doing well. He should wake up soon."

As if on cue, Maya's father stirred, his eyes slowly opening. Maya gasped, squeezing his hand. "Dad!"

He gave her a weak smile. "Hey, kiddo."

Maya's heart leaped with relief and joy. "Dad, you're awake! I was so scared," she said, tears streaming down her face.

"I know, sweetheart," he replied, his voice raspy. "But I'm still here. I'm not going anywhere."

Maya hugged him gently, careful of the tubes and wires. "I love you, Dad."

"I love you too, Maya," he said, his eyes filled with warmth despite his exhaustion.

Liam and his mother watched the touching reunion, their own eyes misty. Liam's mother gently patted Maya's back. "See? He's a fighter, just like you."

Liam smiled, feeling a sense of relief wash over him. "We're all here for you, Mr. Albright. Get well soon."

Maya's father nodded weakly. "Thank you, Liam. And thank you for being here for Maya. It means the world to me."

Liam's mother stepped forward. "Maya, why don't you and Liam go get some fresh air? I'll stay here with your dad."

Maya hesitated but then nodded. "Okay. But I'll be back soon, Dad."

"I'll be right here," he assured her, squeezing her hand weakly but with affection.

Over the next few days, Maya's father slowly recovered. Liam's mother visited often, bringing food and keeping Maya company. One afternoon, she sat down with Maya and the doctor to discuss her father's condition.

"Your father is going to need some time to recover fully," the doctor explained. "He'll need to take it easy for a while."

Liam's mother looked at Maya kindly. "I'm going to help take care of you while your dad is in the hospital, okay?"

Maya nodded, grateful but still worried. "Thank you."

Despite the good news, Maya found it hard to focus on anything other than her father's health. She didn't want to go to school or practice for the show. One evening, she sat by her father's bed, tears in her eyes. "Dad, I can't do it. I can't focus on anything knowing you're here."

Her father reached out and took her hand, his grip weak but warm. "Maya, you need to keep going. I know it's hard, but I want you to continue practicing for the show and going to school."

"But what if something happens to you? What if you..." She couldn't finish the sentence, the thought too painful to voice.

He squeezed her hand gently. "I'm going to be okay. The doctors here are taking good care of me. And I want to see you dance and sing. It's important to me."

Maya sniffed, wiping her tears. "But I'm scared, Dad."

"I know, sweetheart. But you're strong. You've got Liam, Munay, and Lily. They'll help you through this. And I'll be there in spirit, cheering you on."

As if sensing her distress, Munay and Lily, who were brought by Liam's mother to the hospital, meowed softly from their carrier at the foot of the bed. Liam's mother gently released them, and they padded over to Maya, their purring a soothing balm to her frayed nerves.

Liam's mother smiled warmly at Maya. "I thought Munay and Lily might cheer you up. They miss you and your dad, too."

Maya reached down to stroke Munay's fur, the familiar feel comforting her. "Thanks, Mrs. Thompson. They do make me feel better."

Munay nuzzled against Maya's leg, purring loudly. "We're here for you, Maya," he seemed to say.

Lily jumped onto the bed, curling up beside Maya's father. He chuckled weakly, reaching out to pet her. "See? Even the cats know you need to keep going."

Maya took a deep breath, her father's words giving her a new resolve. She knew he was right. She had to keep going, not just for herself but for him too.

The next day, Liam came over to visit. "How's your dad?" he asked gently, his eyes filled with concern.

"He's getting better," Maya replied, managing a small smile. "He told me to keep practicing for the show."

Liam nodded, smiling. "That's great news. And he's right. We've got to make this the best performance ever."

Maya looked at Liam, her eyes determined. "I know we can do it, Liam. For my dad."

Liam grinned, his enthusiasm infectious. "Absolutely. We'll make him proud."

They started their practice sessions again, Liam on the piano and Maya working on her dance moves with Munay and Lily nearby, providing their usual support. Despite her fears, Maya felt a renewed sense of purpose. Every step, every note, was a promise to her father that she would keep going, no matter what.

Chapter XIII: The Trial Performance

The excitement for the end-of-year show grew as the big day approached. Maya and Liam, with Munay and Lily always by their side, practiced tirelessly, determined to make their performance perfect. The official trial performance was set to take place, giving all participants a chance to practice on stage with lights, sound, and everything in between.

On the morning of the trial performance, Maya and Liam arrived at the school auditorium, their hearts pounding with both excitement and nerves. The large room was buzzing with the chatter of students, teachers, and parents, all eager to see the rehearsals. The stage, with its bright lights shining like stars and grand, heavy curtains hanging majestically, loomed before them. It felt both thrilling and intimidating, a place where dreams could come true but also where fears could be magnified. Maya and Liam took deep breaths, trying to steady their racing hearts, ready to face the challenge ahead.

While they were setting up for their practice, some of their classmates, who had always been unkind to Maya, approached them. The leader of the group, a girl named Tricia, smirked as she saw Maya's anxious expression. Tricia had long, straight hair and always wore a mean look on her face. Her friends followed close behind, giggling and whispering.

"Well, well, if it isn't Maya and Liam," Tricia sneered, her voice dripping with sarcasm. "Ready to make fools of yourselves?" She crossed her arms and raised an eyebrow, clearly enjoying making Maya feel nervous. The other kids snickered, making Maya's heart race even faster.

Maya's heart sank, but she stood her ground. Her legs felt wobbly, but she lifted her chin and looked Tricia in the eyes. "We're here to perform, just like everyone else," she said, her voice steady despite the knot of fear in her stomach.

Liam stepped forward, standing by Maya's side. He had a determined look on his face. "Leave us alone, Tricia. We're trying to practice."

Tricia and her friends laughed loudly, their laughter echoing through the auditorium. "Practice?" Tricia sneered, flipping her hair over her shoulder. "You think anyone wants to see a girl who can barely dance and a piano boy? This is going to be hilarious."

Maya felt tears prickling at the corners of her eyes. Her cheeks flushed with embarrassment and frustration. She glanced down at Munay and Lily, who were sitting by the stage. Munay's eyes were fixed on the bullies, his fur bristling slightly. Lily's ears were tilted back, sensing the tension.

Tricia moved closer, her eyes narrowing. She reached out and knocked over Liam's sheet music with a flick of her hand. The papers scattered across the floor. "Oops," Tricia said with a smirk. "Looks like you'll have to pick that up."

Liam clenched his fists, but he stayed calm. "Why are you being so mean?" he asked, his voice firm but hurt. "We haven't done anything to you."

Tricia shrugged, her smile fading. "Because it's fun," she said simply. "Watching you two try to be something you're not is the best entertainment we've had all day."

Maya bent down to pick up the scattered sheet music, her hands shaking. Munay and Lily moved closer. She looked up at Liam, who knelt beside her, helping to gather the papers.

Before Liam could respond, Munay and Lily sprang into action. Munay, with his sleek black fur and determined eyes, hissed loudly, his back arching. Lily, with her striking blue eyes and elegant stance, bared her teeth and let out a fierce growl.

Startled, Tricia and her friends took a step back. "Whoa, keep your cats under control," Tricia stammered, her bravado faltering as she looked nervously at the fierce felines.

Lily advanced, her growl growing louder and more menacing. Munay joined her, his fur bristling. Together, they stood their ground, their united front making them appear larger and more intimidating. The bullies, clearly unnerved, backed away even further.

"Let's get out of here," one of Tricia's friends muttered, tugging at her sleeve.

"Yeah, whatever," Tricia said, trying to sound casual but failing. "This isn't worth it."

The bullies retreated. Maya and Liam exchanged a look of relief and gratitude. Maya knelt down, stroking Munay and Lily with shaky hands. "Thank you," she whispered, her voice thick with emotion. "You were so brave."

Liam nodded, still in awe of the cats' courage. "We couldn't have done it without you two," he said, giving Munay and Lily a gentle pat. The cats purred in response, their eyes shining with pride.

With the bullies gone, Maya and Liam finally had the time and space they needed to practice properly. They ran through their routine, Maya dancing while Liam played the piano. Munay and Lily stayed close, their presence a comforting reminder of their support.

"We can finally focus," Liam said, setting up his sheet music. "No more distractions."

Maya nodded, smiling. "Let's show everyone what we can do."

They began their practice, and the stage felt less intimidating. Maya found her confidence growing with each step and note. She focused on her strengths, using graceful arm movements and twirls that highlighted her abilities rather than her limitations. Liam's music was the perfect accompaniment, his fingers moving skillfully across the keys.

At one point, Maya stumbled slightly, her leg giving her trouble. She looked down, worried that she might not be able to continue. Munay, sensing her distress, leaped onto the stage and began to dance beside her, using his paws to mimic her movements. Lily joined in, their playful antics bringing a smile to Maya's face.

"Look, Maya," Liam said, his voice filled with encouragement. "Munay and Lily are dancing with you. They're not letting anything stop them, and neither should you."

Maya took a deep breath, drawing strength from her furry friends' determination. "You're right, Liam. We can do this."

They continued their practice, the music filling the auditorium with a sense of hope and resilience. Munay and Lily's presence added a unique charm to their performance, making it truly special.

On the afternoon, it was time for their official trial performance, the auditorium was filled only with students, teachers and the journalist from the local city newspaper who took pictures for the invitations to the school show in the next paper edition of tomorrow. The anticipation was palpable as they took their places on stage.

"I'm a little nervous," Maya admitted, glancing at Liam.

"We've got this," Liam said, nodding reassuringly. "Just

remember our practice."

Maya took a deep breath and began to sing, her voice clear and strong. Liam's piano playing was flawless, each note perfectly complementing her vocals.

While Maya was dancing, she felt the familiar twinge in her leg, but instead of letting it stop her, she adapted her movements, using her hands and arms to convey the emotion of the song. Munay and Lily joined in, their playful movements adding a touch of magic to the performance.

The audience watched in awe, captivated by the beauty and strength of their routine. When they finished, the auditorium exploded in joyous applause. Maya and Liam exchanged a look of triumph, their hearts soaring with pride and relief.

Backstage, Maya hugged Munay and Lily, her gratitude overflowing. "Thank you, Munay. Thank you, Lily. We did it!"

Liam smiled, his eyes shining with happiness. "We really did. And it's all thanks to you two," he said, giving the cats a gentle pat.

The trial performance was a success, boosting Maya and Liam's confidence. They knew that with Munay and Lily by their side, they could overcome any obstacle. The end-of-year show was just around the corner, and they were ready to shine.

Maya felt a renewed sense of determination as they left the auditorium, ready to face whatever challenges lay ahead with the support of her friends, both human and feline. With the show drawing near, they continued to practice, their bond growing stronger each day.

Despite the bullies' attempts to bring them down, Maya and Liam knew they were unstoppable. They had each other, they had Munay and Lily, and they had the courage to overcome any obstacle. The end-of-year show would be their moment to shine, a testament to their resilience and friendship. However, as they practiced, Maya couldn't help but think about her father, still in the hospital recovering from his surgery. The joy of their successful rehearsal was tinged with sadness and worry, knowing her father might not be able to attend the show.

"I wish Dad could be there," Maya said softly to Liam one afternoon. "It's hard to focus on being happy when I'm so worried about him."

Liam gave her a reassuring smile. "He'd want you to keep going, Maya. He'd be so proud of you. And we'll record the performance for him to see when he gets better." Maya nodded, feeling a mix of determination and sorrow, knowing she had to keep going for her father's sake as well as her own.

Chapter XIV: A Song of Hope

The end-of-year show began with an air of excitement that filled the auditorium like a charged electric buzz. Students poured into the space, their chatter echoing off the walls as they found their seats. Teachers bustled about, ensuring everything was in order, while the stage crew made final adjustments to the lighting and props.

The stage itself was an amazing sight, decorated with colorful lights that danced across the curtains drawn in anticipation of the performances. The atmosphere buzzed with energy, each person in the audience eagerly awaiting the spectacle about to unfold.

As the show commenced, one by one, teams of performers took the stage, each group showcasing their unique talents and skills. There were singers with voices that soared like birds in flight, dancers whose movements were as graceful as swaying trees in the wind, musicians who filled the air with beautiful melodies that stirred the soul, and even a group of acrobats whose daring feats left the audience breathless with awe.

Among the audience, whispers of admiration and excitement filled the air as students and teachers alike marveled at the creativity and dedication displayed by their peers. "Did you see that dance routine?" one student exclaimed to their friend, their eyes wide with wonder. "It was like something out of a movie!"

Near the back of the auditorium, the stage crew worked tirelessly to ensure the smooth running of the show. "Lights dimmed, check!" called out one crew member with an excited voice. "Sound levels set, check!" chimed in another, a sense of pride evident in their tone.

Meanwhile, teachers and staff members mingled with the

audience, their smiles reflecting the joy and anticipation of the moment. "I can't wait to see what our students have prepared," remarked one teacher to a colleague, their eyes shining with pride. "They've put in so much hard work and dedication."

The auditorium buzzed with anticipation as the first act took the stage. A group of kids, their faces beaming with nervous excitement, launched into a lively dance routine. Their movements were a kaleidoscope of color, their costumes sparkling under the stage lights. As their synchronized steps filled the air, a wave of laughter rippled through the audience. Parents cheered, friends whooped, and everyone clapped along to the upbeat music.

Next came a group of singers, their voices blending in perfect harmony. Their song, filled with joy and optimism, washed over the audience like a warm wave. Heads swayed back and forth, and a few students even hummed along, their faces lit up with a touch of magic.

The energy in the room was electric! After each performance, loud cheers erupted, punctuated by joyous shouts of "Bravo! Bravo!" The sense of camaraderie was palpable – everyone was there to support each other, to celebrate their friends' talents, and to revel in the shared experience. It was truly a night to remember, a testament to the power of friendship, creativity, and having fun together.

Maya and Liam waited backstage, their tummies full of jittery butterflies. Maya's heart thumped like a drum solo in her chest. She took a deep breath, trying to smell the calming scent of the pretty flowers nearby.

Liam, her best friend, knew she was nervous. He flashed her a big smile. "You'll be amazing, Maya! Just breathe and enjoy the show!"

Maya nodded, feeling better with Liam by her side. She closed her eyes and thought about their song. It always made her feel brave. The words talked about hope and not giving up, and that made her tummy feel a little less fluttery.

"Showtime!" announced the stage manager. Maya's worry Evaporated like mist in the morning sun. She and Liam walked onto the stage together, Munay and Lily following close behind, looking super proud.

The crowd clapped and cheered. Maya took a big breath and started to sing. Her voice, clear and sweet, filled the room:

"In the shadows, I once stood,

Feeling lost and misunderstood.

With every step, I faced the fall,

But I found strength to stand tall."

Liam's fingers flew across the piano keys like tiny dancers, creating a beautiful melody that intertwined perfectly with Maya's singing. The music flowed through the auditorium, filling the room with a warm, happy feeling, like sunshine on a summer day.

Maya sang her heart out, putting all her emotions into each word. Her voice was strong and clear, reaching every corner of the room. It sounded beautiful, filled with feeling and honesty. Munay and Lily stood next to her on stage, watching their friend with big, proud eyes. They loved hearing Maya sing!

As Maya sang the chorus, the music filled the air, making everyone feel excited. Maya couldn't help but move to the beat, swaying gently from side to side. Munay and Lily joined in, dancing around her with their tails swishing happily.

Maya's movements were graceful, like a bird flying in the

sky. She waved her arms and twirled around, feeling the music in her heart. Munay and Lily followed her lead, jumping and spinning with joy.

Together, they danced to the rhythm of the song, their movements telling a story of courage and strength. The audience watched in awe, amazed by Maya's talent and the beauty of their performance, while Maya continues:

"In the shadows, hear my voice,

Your words will disappear, your memories will disappear.

Loved ones' strength will keep me strong,

In their love, I now belong."

The chorus echoed through the auditorium touched everyone's hearts. Maya's voice soared, carrying the message of hope and resilience to all who listened.

When the song reached its climax, Maya's father arrived at the auditorium, just in time to see his daughter perform. Tears welled up in his eyes as he watched Maya on stage, her voice filling the room with its beauty and strength.

Maya's heart swelled with emotion as she caught sight of her father in the audience. She sang with even more passion and determination, wanting to make him proud.

"My mother's love, my father's pride,

In my heart, they will reside.

With Minoush by my side,

Together, we will ride."

The words flowed easily from Maya's lips, each line carrying the weight of her love and gratitude for her parents and her friends. Munay and Lily watched from the wings, their hearts filled with love and admiration for their brave friend.

"Overcoming every trial,

With a hopeful, grateful smile.
The stage is set, the future bright,
I'll keep singing through the night."

When the final notes of the song rang out, the audience erupted into loud cheers. The auditorium was filled with the sound of cheering and clapping. Maya and Liam took a bow, their faces flushed with excitement and joy. Munay and Lily joined them on stage, their tails wagging with pride.

The teachers were beaming with pride, nodding and clapping enthusiastically. Mrs. Bennett, their music teacher, had tears in her eyes. She whispered to the teacher next to her, "They've worked so hard for this. What an incredible performance."

The pupils were equally enthusiastic, standing on their feet, cheering loudly. Even the bullies, including Tricia, seemed taken aback. They looked at each other with a mixture of surprise and respect. Tricia, unable to hide her admiration, muttered, "That was actually pretty amazing."

In the front row, Maya's father and Liam's mother were standing, clapping the loudest of all. Tears streamed down Maya's father's cheeks as he watched his daughter shine on stage. Liam's mother had a proud, beaming smile on her face, her eyes glistening with joy.

When the applause began to die down, the principal stepped onto the stage, holding a microphone. "Ladies and gentlemen, what a fantastic performance! Let's give another round of applause for Maya, Liam, Munay, and Lily!"

The audience cheered once more, and Maya and Liam exchanged joyful glances. Munay and Lily meowed softly, actually, the applause was for them too.

"And now," the principal continued, "it's time for the awards announcement. We have seen some amazing skills today, but one performance stood out for its creativity, heart, and determination. The first award goes to... Maya, Liam, and their amazing cats, Munay and Lily!"

The auditorium exploded with applause and cheers. Maya and Liam's faces lit up shocked with joy. They exchanged looks of disbelief and then joy. Munay and Lily purred loudly, rubbing against Maya's and Liam's legs.

Mrs. Johnson came forward, holding a shiny trophy. "Maya, Liam, Munay, and Lily, this is for you. You showed us all the power of perseverance and friendship."

Maya accepted the trophy with shaky hands. "Thank you so much," she said, her voice full of emotion. "We couldn't have done it without all of you believing in us."

The principal smiled warmly. "Your performance reminded us all of the power of friendship and the strength that comes from believing in oneself. Congratulations!"

Maya and Liam turned to each other, holding the trophy between them, their hearts overflowing with happiness. They knelt down, hugging Munay and Lily, who seemed to bask in the applause and attention.

The ceremony is concluded and the audience began to leave the auditorium. Maya's father rushed forward, tears streaming down his cheeks. "Maya, that was incredible," he said, pulling her into a tight hug. "I'm so proud of you."

Maya hugged him back, her heart overflowing with happiness. "Thank you, Dad," she whispered. "I couldn't have done it without you."

Liam's mother joined them, hugging Liam tightly. "You

were fantastic, Liam. I'm so proud of you," she said, her voice choked with emotion.

At that moment, Maya's father felt a tap on their shoulders. Turning around, he saw two unfamiliar faces approaching – Hannah and Tom, accompanied by their parents. Munay's heart skipped a beat as he realized who they were. Munay and Lily exchanged surprised glances, clearly taken aback by the unexpected appearance of their friends from the farm.

Chapter XV: Goodbye

"**Hi** there," Mr. Henderson greeted warmly, extending his hand. "I'm Mr. Henderson, and this is my wife. These are our children, Hannah and Tom. We couldn't miss the opportunity to see this wonderful performance."

Maya's father and Liam's mother shook hands with Mr. and Mrs. Henderson, their faces showing a mix of surprise and curiosity. "I am sorry, but, have we met before?" Maya's father asked. He was curious.

Mr. Henderson let out a hearty chuckle. "No! we saw an invitation for the show in the local newspaper. There was a picture of Maya with Munay and Lily, and we recognized the cats immediately. The cats were missing for a couple of months. So, we decided to come and see for ourselves."

Munay and Lily, who had been enjoying the attention from the crowd, suddenly felt a mix of emotions wash over them. They were thrilled to see the familiar faces of their old family but couldn't shake the fear of potentially losing Maya and Liam.

Maya's father nodded, understanding dawning on his face. "I see. Well, Maya and Liam found Munay and Lily in the city streets. They've taken very good care of them."

Despite the fact that Hannah and Tom were at first super excited to have Munay around and played with him all the time, once summer vacation ended, they had to go back to school. School kept them busy with lessons and hanging out with friends, so they didn't have as much time to play with Munay anymore.

As for Lily, well, the neighbor who used to live next door wasn't a big fan of cats, so she spent most of her time with the other farm animals. Yet, as Hannah and Tom were amazed by the performance they had just witnessed, they looked eagerly at their father. "Can we take them back home, Daddy? We've missed them so much!"

Maya's father could feel the weight of the situation pressing down on him. He knew how much Munay and Lily meant to Maya and Liam. "Why don't we go back to our house and talk about this?" he suggested. "We need to figure out what's best for everyone."

The Hendersons agreed, and they all began the walk to Maya's home. As they walked, the children chattered excitedly about the performance, praising Munay and Lily's amazing talents. Munay and Lily followed along, their tails flicking nervously, sensing the importance of the conversation.

Once they arrived at Maya's house, everyone settled into the living room. Munay and Lily curled up on the rug, watching the humans with wide, curious eyes. Maya's father started the conversation.

"I understand that Munay and Lily were part of your family first, and I can see how much they mean to Hannah and Tom," he began. "But I also need you to understand how much they mean to Maya and Liam. These past few months, they've brought so much joy and comfort into their lives."

Mr. Henderson nodded. "I do understand. We saw how well they performed tonight, and it's clear they've been loved and cared for."

Mr. Henderson sighed and added, "My kids cannot do much about the situation now, but we'd like to take the cats back to the farm where they belong."

Maya's father nodded, his heart heavy. "I understand. Let me talk to Maya, and Liam's mother will talk to him. We'll explain everything."

While the kids played together with the cats, Maya's father and Liam's mother approached them. "Maya, Liam," they called softly, "we need to talk to you inside."

The children exchanged puzzled looks but followed their parents inside. Maya's father knelt down to her level, his eyes filled with sadness. "Maya, sweetie, we need to talk about Munay and Lily. It seems their original owners have come to find them."

Liam's mother added gently, "Mr. Henderson and his family miss Munay and Lily very much. They've come all the way here because they saw the invitation in the newspaper."

Tears welled up in Maya's eyes as she clung to her father. "But they're our cats now! We've taken care of them and love them so much!"

Liam, his eyes brimming with tears, nodded. "We can't lose them now. They're part of our family."

Maya's father hugged her tightly. "I know, sweetheart. But we have to do what's right. Munay and Lily were theirs first, and they have missed them terribly."

Liam's mother explained softly, "It's not easy, but sometimes we have to let go of things we love. We can still visit them, and who knows, maybe one day you'll have your own pets again."

Maya and Liam sobbed, clinging to their parents. The weight of the situation was too much for their young hearts to bear. Munay and Lily, sensing the distress, rubbed against their legs, trying to offer comfort.

Maya and Liam sobbed, clinging to their parents.

The weight of the situation was too much for their young

hearts to bear. Munay and Lily, sensing the distress, rubbed against their legs, trying to offer comfort.

Maya pulled away and ran to her room, slamming the door behind her. She threw herself onto her bed, her sobs echoing through the house. "It's not fair!" she cried into her pillow, her tears soaking the fabric. "I don't want them to go! They're our family now!"

Liam, tears streaming down his own cheeks, looked up at his mother with a mix of confusion and heartbreak. "Why do they have to leave? Can't they stay with us?"

Liam's mother knelt beside him, her voice soothing but sad. "I know it hurts, Liam. But sometimes we have to do what's right, even when it's hard. Munay and Lily were their cats first, and they missed them just as much as you love them now."

Maya's father gently knocked on her door before entering. He sat beside her on the bed, rubbing her back. "I know this is incredibly hard, Maya. But we have to think about what's best for Munay and Lily too. They have a family that loves them and misses them."

Maya looked up at her father, her eyes red and puffy. "But we love them too, Dad. They belong with us."

"I know, sweetheart," he said softly. "And they will always be a part of our hearts. But Mr. Henderson's family has missed them so much. Maybe one day, you can visit them at the farm."

After a long while, Maya took a deep breath, wiping her tears. She stood up, her legs shaky but determined. "Okay," she whispered. "I want to say goodbye."

With heavy hearts, Maya and Liam gathered Munay and Lily in their arms one last time. The cats, sensing the seriousness of the moment, snuggled close, their purrs a comforting hum against the children's chests.

"Goodbye, Munay and Lily," Maya whispered, her voice breaking as she kissed Munay's head. "We'll miss you so much. Be happy at the farm."

Liam hugged Munay tightly, his small arms trembling. "Munay, Lily, we love you. We'll never forget you."

Tears streamed down both their cheeks as they reluctantly handed the cats to Mr. Henderson. Munay and Lily let out soft meows, their own form of goodbye.

The Hendersons gathered their things and prepared to leave. Munay and Lily, looking back one last time, let out soft meows, as if to say goodbye.

When the Hendersons drove away in their pickup truck, Maya and Liam watched from the window, their hearts aching. Munay and Lily, peeking out from the back seat of the truck, pressed their little noses against the glass, their eyes wide and sad. Their ears perked up, as if they were trying to understand why they were leaving their beloved new family.

Maya and Liam waved frantically, their hands trembling, tears streaming down their faces. "Goodbye, Munay! Goodbye, Lily!" they called out, their voices choked with emotion. The cats meowed softly in response, their eyes reflecting their own sense of loss and confusion.

The truck slowly drove down the road but Munay's gaze remained locked on Maya and Liam until they were out of sight. Lily, too, kept turning her head back, her tail flicking anxiously. The distance grew, and the children felt the separation more with each passing second.

Maya's heart pounded as she pressed her forehead against

the window, trying to capture every last glimpse of the departing truck. "I hope they'll be okay," she whispered, her voice breaking.

Liam stood beside her, his small frame shaking with sobs. "I already miss them so much," he said, his voice barely audible.

The truck finally disappeared from sight, and the reality of the situation sank in. The children slowly turned away from the window, their shoulders heavy with the weight of their grief. The house felt emptier without Munay and Lily, the silence echoing the void left by their absence.

Munay and Lily, nestled in the back of the truck, curled up together for comfort. Munay's mismatched eyes looked up at the sky, as if searching for the familiar faces of Maya and Liam. Lily gently licked Munay's head, trying to soothe him, but her own eyes were filled with sadness.

The truck drove further away, Maya and Liam hugged each other tightly, finding comfort in their shared pain, and hoping that Munay and Lily would find happiness back at the farm.

Maya and Liam spent the rest of the evening in quiet reflection, the memories of their time with Munay and Lily flooding their minds. They whispered to each other about the funny moments, the cuddles, and the way Munay would always purr loudly when he was happy.

The night was long, and sleep came slowly, but in their dreams, they saw Munay and Lily, happy and playing, surrounded by the love of both their families. It was a bittersweet comfort, a reminder that love could stretch across any distance, no matter how far apart they were.

Chapter XVI: Love Means Letting Go

Back on the farm, life seemed to carry on as usual. The sun rose and set over the fields that stretched out as far as the eye could see. Golden waves of wheat swayed gently in the breeze, while rows of vegetables grew neatly in the rich, dark soil. The barn stood tall and weathered, a familiar landmark amidst the greenery. The animals roamed freely, cows lazily grazed in the pasture, their gentle lowing blending with the clucking of chickens scratching the dirt for feed. Horses neighed softly as they trotted around the paddock, their manes glistening in the sunlight. The air was filled with the fresh scent of hay and the sweet fragrance of blooming wildflowers, and the sounds of birds chirping from the trees created a symphony of rural life.

Despite the idyllic surroundings, everyone appeared happy—everyone except for Munay and Lily. The two cats missed their friends Liam and Maya terribly, and it showed. Munay often sat by the edge of the field, staring off into the distance, his ears perked up at the faintest sound, hoping it might be his friends coming to find him. His once lively spirit seemed dimmed, and his usual playfulness was replaced with a quiet, somber demeanor. Lily, too, wandered the farm with a sense of loss, often curling up in hidden corners of the barn, away from the other animals, longing for the familiar warmth and comfort of Maya's and Liam's company.

Hannah and Tom, still amazed by Munay's performance on stage, tried to make him dance again. "Come on, Munay! Dance like you did with Maya!" Hannah urged, clapping her hands excitedly.

Tom waved a feather toy in front of Munay. "You can do it, Munay! Just like in the show!"

But Munay just stared at them, his deep blue eyes filled with sorrow. He didn't understand why they wanted him to dance now. Dancing had been something special he did to make Maya happy. Without her, it felt meaningless.

"Why won't he dance?" Hannah pouted, lowering the feather toy.

Their father, Mr. Henderson, sighed as he watched the scene unfold. "Munay danced for Maya because he loved her and wanted to make her happy. He doesn't understand why he should dance now."

Days passed, and Munay and Lily still refused to eat much of the food they were given. They ignored the playful antics of the other animals and spent most of their time lying in the barn, their tails barely flicking in response to any attempts to cheer them up. Hannah and Tom, busy with school and friends, soon stopped trying to get Munay to dance and paid little attention to the cats.

Meanwhile, back in the city, Maya and Liam were struggling with the absence of their beloved pets. Their home felt emptier without Munay and Lily. The laughter that used to fill the house was replaced by a heavy silence.

Maya would often sit on her bed, clutching Munay's favorite blanket. "I miss them so much, Dad," she whispered, tears welling up in her eyes. "It feels like a part of me is missing."

Her father sat beside her, wrapping his arm around her shoulders. "I know, sweetie. I miss them too. They were special to us."

Liam spent his days staring out the window, hoping for a miracle. "Do you think Munay and Lily are okay, Mom?" he asked one evening, his voice trembling.

Liam's mother knelt beside him, holding his hand. "I'm sure they are, Liam. But it's okay to miss them and feel sad. They were a big part of our lives."

As the days went by, both the cats and the children struggled with their emotions. Munay and Lily's condition didn't improve, and their refusal to eat or play worried Mr. and Mrs. Henderson more each day.

One afternoon, as the sun was setting, Hannah found Munay lying on a bale of hay, looking more miserable than ever. "What's wrong, Munay?" she asked softly, stroking his fur. "Why won't you be happy here?"

Munay looked up at her with his deep blue eyes, a silent plea for understanding. He missed the warmth of Maya's embrace, the sound of Liam's laughter, and the feeling of being truly loved.

Tom noticed Lily curled up in a corner, refusing to interact with the other animals. He approached her slowly, sitting down beside her. "Lily, we love you too," he said quietly. "But I can see you're not happy here. What can we do to make it better?"

The Hendersons watched the once lively kittens turn into shadows of their former selves. They began to understand that love couldn't be forced. Munay and Lily needed Maya and Liam just as much as the children needed them.

The realization hit hard, and the Hendersons knew they had a difficult decision to make. They couldn't bear to see the cats suffer any longer, and it became clear that their happiness lay elsewhere. The farm, despite its beauty and comfort, wasn't their true home anymore. Munay and Lily's hearts belonged with Maya and Liam.

Chapter XVII: Where Love Resides

One evening, as the family gathered for dinner, Mr. Henderson cleared his throat and spoke gently to wife, his brow furrowed with concern. "Maybe we need to talk to the owner of Lily and see what they think. It's clear that Munay and Lily aren't happy here," he said, his voice heavy with worry.

Mrs. Henderson nodded thoughtfully, her eyes reflecting the same concern. "You're right. They seemed so much happier with Maya and Liam. We owe it to them to make sure they're where they're loved and cared for the most."

Later that evening, they gathered Tom and Hannah in the cozy living room. The fire crackled in the hearth, casting a warm glow around the room. Mr. Henderson began, "Kids, we need to talk about Munay and Lily. We've noticed that they aren't as happy as they used to be. I believe that they miss Maya and Liam."

Tom looked down at his shoes, guilt flickering in his eyes. "Yeah, Dad. I've tried to play with Munay, but he just isn't the same. He won't dance like he used to."

Hannah added, "And Lily doesn't purr or cuddle like she did when we first brought her home. They're always staring out the window, like they're waiting for someone."

Mr. Henderson glanced at his wife, who nodded in encouragement. "We've been thinking, maybe it's best for Munay and Lily to go back to Maya and Liam. They've been through a lot together, and it's clear they have a special bond."

Tom's eyes welled up with tears. "But we've missed them too, Dad. They were our pets first."

Mrs. Henderson leaned forward, her voice gentle. "I know, sweetheart. But sometimes, the best way to show love is to let go. Munay and Lily found a new family with Maya and Liam, a family that loves them deeply. And you'll always have the memories you shared."

Hannah sniffled, wiping her tears. "Can we at least visit them sometimes?"

Mr. Henderson smiled softly. "Of course. We can visit them. And who knows, maybe you'll find other animals who need your love and care just as much."

After some thoughtful discussions, with everyone sharing their feelings and memories, they all agreed that Munay and Lily would be happier with their new friends. The next day, they all prepared for the drive back to the city. The decision was hard, but it was the right thing to do for the happiness of the cats.

When they packed up the truck, Tom and Hannah gave Munay and Lily one last hug. "We love you, Munay and Lily. Be happy," Tom whispered, his voice breaking.

Hannah kissed Munay on the head. "We'll never forget you. Have fun with Maya and Liam."

Mr. Henderson looked at his children with pride and sadness. "You're doing the right thing, kids. It's not easy, but it's the right thing."

The drive back to the city was filled with mixed emotions, but there was a sense of peace knowing that Munay and Lily would be back where they belonged, with the friends who loved them the most.

Meanwhile, back in the city, Maya felt a very strong sense of loneliness settle over her like a heavy blanket. Each day seemed to stretch endlessly, the rain adding a gloomy view to her somber mood. She would sit by the window for hours, watching the droplets cascade down the glass, her thoughts filled by memories of Munay's playful antics and Lily's gentle purrs.

On one particularly gloomy afternoon, the heavy rain was hiding the world outside in a blurry haze. Maya's gaze was fixed on the downpour, lost in her own thoughts, when a distant rumble caught her attention. Peering through the rain-streaked glass, her heart leaped with excitement as she saw a familiar pickup truck approaching through the mist.

"DAD! They're back!" Maya's voice echoed through the house, bursting with pure joy. Without a second thought, she bounded towards the front door, her steps quick and eager.

When she opened the door, a rush of cold, damp air greeted her, mingling with the warm scent of rain-soaked earth. Standing out against the storm's fury, a beacon of hope emerged in the form of Mr. Henderson and his family, their smiles radiating warmth even through the downpour. And there, curled up between them, were Munay and Lily, their fur damp but their eyes bright with happiness.

Running into the front yard, she embraced Munay and Lily, her heart bursting with happiness. The rain soaked her hair and clothes, but she didn't care. From the neighboring house, Liam spotted the scene and sprinted over, his eyes wide with disbelief and joy.

Together, they held Munay and Lily in their arms, the rain pouring down around them. Their reunion was a radiant sun breaking through the storm's gloomy sky. Their laughter and tears of joy mixed with the sound of the falling rain.

All the parents stood at the doorway, watching the beautiful scene unfold. They exchanged knowing smiles, their hearts lightened by the sight of their children's pure happiness.

Munay and Lily curled up comfortably in the arms of their friends, purring contentedly. Despite the chilly rain, the warmth of love and friendship enveloped them, just like it did the first time Maya and Liam had taken them in, protecting them from the cold.

In that moment, everyone understood that home wasn't just a place, but the people who filled it with love and care. Munay and Lily were finally home. It is love, kindness, and shared memories that make a place feel like home. The rain may have fallen around them, but in their hearts, there was nothing but sunshine.

H&M Publishers – 2024

THE END

Acknowledgments

I am deeply grateful to my wife and children for their patience and understanding, allowing me the time and space to bring this story to life. Your encouragement and belief in me have been a constant source of inspiration.

A special thank you to my wife for her invaluable help with the finishing touches of the story and the illustrations. Your creativity and dedication have brought my vision to life in ways I could not have achieved alone.

I also wish to express my heartfelt thanks to my colleagues, friends, and students. Your support and encouragement, as well as your contributions to the illustrations and digital editing, have been instrumental in the creation of this book. Your collaborative spirit and enthusiasm have made this project a reality.

Thank you all for being part of this journey and for helping make this book possible.

H&M Publishers – 2024

About the Author

H. BEN MEKKI is a passionate educator and author who empowers students to master English and French while coaching them toward success. He also writes children's and young adult books, bringing engaging stories to life.